BUDDY AND BEA
Tiny Tornadoes

For Nancy Cabrero, Liz Furey-Jablonski, Marjorie Martinelli, and all teachers who are comfortable with a little classroom chaos.

–J.C.

For the kids, George, Cammy, Peter, Camille, Dilly, Francie, Ori, and Lee.

–K.M.

Published by
PEACHTREE PUBLISHING COMPANY INC.
1700 Chattahoochee Avenue
Atlanta, Georgia 30318-2112
PeachtreeBooks.com

Text © 2023 by Jan Carr
Illustrations © 2023 by Kris Mukai

Edited by Catherine Frank
Design and composition by Lily Steele
The illustrations were rendered digitally.

Printed and bound in May 2023 at Lake Book Manufacturing, Melrose Park, IL, USA
10 9 8 7 6 5 4 3 2 1
First Edition
ISBN: 978-1-68263-535-3

Cataloging-in-Publication Data is available from the Library of Congress.

BUDDY AND BEA
Tiny Tornadoes

Jan Carr
Illustrated by Kris Mukai

PEACHTREE
ATLANTA

CONTENTS

CHAPTER ONE
Mystery Mess

Buddy said goodbye to Poppy just outside school. Inside, he said good morning to Ms. King, the safety agent. Then he marched past the office on the way to his classroom. Ms. Flores waved to him.

"How's my best Buddy?" she asked.

"Great!" he said. He gave a thumbs-up.

Now that he was in second grade, everybody knew him. Even the principal! And it was still only the very first week! The last day of the first week, but still. He'd accomplished all this by Friday!

Buddy really liked the people in his school. Mostly. Because they really liked him. But there were a few people he was still getting used to. Because they were new. Like his teacher, Ms. Maple. And that new girl, Bea.

Buddy spied Bea ahead of him in the hallway. She was talking to someone. It was Jabari, another second-grade teacher. But he wasn't *their* teacher. Why was Bea talking to Jabari?

Buddy tried to sneak past. He didn't want Bea to see him. She'd want to glom onto him.

But Bea caught up.

"Hey," she said. "My Buddy."

When Ms. Flores called him her buddy, Buddy liked it. But when Bea said it, it felt too sticky. She thought he was her buddy. But he wasn't.

"I'm not your buddy," he said.

"I know," she said. "But your *name* is Buddy. So I like to think of you as *mine*."

And that was the problem. Exactly.

"So guess what?" said Bea. "I told Jabari all about you."

Buddy stopped. He stared at her. "What do you mean?"

"I told him you want to do bird-watching. Like he does." Bea hadn't really done that, had she? "I told him you want to use his *binoculars*."

"Why did you say that?" said Buddy.

"Because I told him you wish you were in his class," said Bea. "So I had to explain *why*."

Buddy's face burned. "You told him *I want to be in his class*?"

"Well, you do," said Bea. "Don't you? You *said*."

What kind of blabbermouth was Bea anyway? One who'd blab every single thing he ever told her?

Buddy sped up to get away. But Bea got to the door of the classroom right as he did. She pushed in front of him.

Buddy put his foot out to block her. But Bea bumped him with her hip, knocking him out of the way.

"Hey!" cried Buddy. "No pushing!"

"I wasn't pushing!" she said. "It was a hip bump. Like a fist bump. But with hips!"

Inside the classroom, Buddy spied Joey, his best friend. Joey and the other kids were huddled together. Something was wrong. The classroom was a mess. A huge mess.

"Whoa," said Bea, looking around. "This place is a *disaster*. It looks like *a tornado* hit it."

It was true. It did. Like a tornado had come through and blown all the books around. Books were everywhere. Scattered on every table. And all across the floor. Buddy had to step around them as he walked in.

A little shiver shot through him. A shiver of excitement. A mess! thought Buddy. A glorious mess!

Sometimes, Buddy liked messes. They made him feel, well . . . fizzy. At home, Buddy liked to take out his action figures and scatter them all over the bed. All over *everywhere*! That felt like his toys had come out to play with him.

Messes could feel *friendly*.

But this wasn't his bedroom. This was his *classroom*.

Buddy walked over to his friends. Joey gestured at the room. "Look!" he said. His eyes were wide, like they were saying, *Wow!*

"Can you believe this?" said Malik.

"What happened?" said Omar.

Their teacher was across the room. Why wasn't she doing anything? *Saying* anything? Would she yell? Buddy couldn't imagine it exactly. He hadn't seen her yell. Not yet. But every teacher got angry. Sometimes.

"Ms. Maple's going to be mad," he said.

"Who made this mess?" asked Joey.

Buddy and his friends looked at Bea.

"You!" said Joey. He pointed at her. "I bet you did it!"

That made sense. Bea was the perfect suspect. There was always a lot of mess around Bea. So Buddy pointed, too.

"Me?" said Bea. "How could I do it? I just got here!"

That was true. Bea had come in the room right when Buddy had. Still, it was the kind of thing she *would* have done. If she could have.

The mess was a mystery.

Ms. Maple called the class to their morning meeting. They gathered on the rug. "Good morning, Class 2–108," she said.

All the kids raised their hands. Though, they didn't wait to get called on.

"Who did this?" asked Priya.

"Who's going to clean it up?" asked Bea.

"Is someone *in trouble*?" asked Buddy.

Ms. Maple waited for everyone to calm down. And then she said, "It was me. I did it."

What?

Whoa! Ms. Maple?

Why?

CHAPTER TWO
Bea's Books

Buddy sat up straighter. He still didn't know Ms. Maple very well. He couldn't tell yet what kind of teacher she was. An *unpredictable* one? The kind of teacher who you never knew *what in the world she might do*?

"I took all the books out of the classroom book baskets," she said. "The baskets that were here from last year. Then I mixed the books up and scattered them all around the room."

Priya waved her hand harder. She asked the question every other kid was thinking. "*Why?*"

"Because now *you* all are going to sort them," said Ms. Maple.

"*But,*" said Priya. She paused. Like she was trying to figure out a way to be polite. "That doesn't make sense, right? The books were already sorted. So why do we have to sort them all over again?"

"Excellent question," said Ms. Maple. "Because when *you* sort the books, you'll get to know them. You'll see all the different books we have in our classroom library. Then, when you want to choose a book, you'll know where to look."

Wow, thought Buddy. Ms. Maple didn't only make messes. She made *sneaky* messes. Which was even more impressive.

Ms. Maple showed them the empty baskets for the books. Each one had a label. Like *Biographies*. Or *Humor*. Or *Space*.

There were a lot of baskets. But Class 2–108 had a lot of kids. So they divided up the labels and the work. And they all got busy.

Omar searched for graphic novels.

Keiko looked for poetry books.

Marisol and Tamar looked for stories about friends.

And Amber collected books about African Americans. She collected a tall stack.

Joey had been gathering books about sports. Then he

looked at Amber's stack. She had a lot of books about people like her. Which made him wonder. Could he find books about kids who used wheelchairs?

"Hey!" Joey called out. "If anyone finds a book with someone who uses a wheelchair, give it here!" He found another book about sports. He put it in his pile. "And if anyone finds a book with sports *and* a wheelchair?" he said. "*Definitely* give it here!"

But Buddy? He hadn't started sorting yet. Sometimes it took Buddy a while to start a project. At home, his dads called him poky. That was because he liked to do things carefully. He liked to *think about* things.

Buddy picked up a book. It had a boy on the cover. Then he picked up another book. It had a different boy. He waggled the books, as if the boys were talking to each other. "I'm a superhero," said the first one. The other boy answered, "Me, too! Let's save the world!" Like they were action figures. Cool!

Bea plopped down next to Buddy. "What are you collecting?" she asked.

Buddy cupped his books to his chest. In case Bea tried

to grab them. She could be grabby. And fast. "What are *you* collecting?" he asked.

Bea held up a basket. She ripped off the old label: *Mysteries*. Then she dropped a book in the basket. It was a book about shark attacks. "Get it?" she asked. "Do you get my category?"

"Books about sharks?" he said.

"No," said Bea. "It's *easy*. Come on."

"Ocean stuff?"

"No!" said Bea. "Think!"

Buddy shrugged.

"Books I want to read!" she said. "Me! Bea!"

She flipped over the label and wrote on the other side:

Bea's Books. Then she taped it back on the basket.

There weren't many books in Bea's basket. So she jumped up to look at Omar's stack. On top was a graphic novel. The cover showed a girl roller-skating.

Bea fanned some other books in front of her. Random

books. As if they were cards she was holding in a card game. "Do you have any books about roller-skating?" she asked Omar. He held up the book on top. Bea grabbed it.

"Hey!" cried Omar. He tried to grab it back.

"Come on!" said Bea. "You have to *play*! It's a *game*. Like Go Fish!"

Then she looked at Priya's pile. On top was a book with planets talking to each other.

"Do you have any books with speech balloons?" asked Bea.

Priya tried her best to shield her book. But somehow Bea snatched it.

Priya scowled. She put her hands on her hips. Then she tattled.

"Ms. Maple!" she called out. "Bea's taking everyone's books!"

Ms. Maple glanced at the clock. "Class 2–108!" she called. "Time to come back to the rug. Let's take a look at the books you've sorted so far."

CHAPTER THREE
A Little Bit of Chaos

The kids grabbed their books and crushed onto the rug. Ms. Maple gave everyone a chance to explain their categories. But Buddy got a little confused. Because some books could fit in more than one category. Kaveh had a book that was a funny book. So it could go in the *Humor* basket. But it was also a book about astronauts. Hmm. So, *Space*? That one was tricky.

Amber showed a book for the African American basket.

"But it's a graphic novel," said Omar.

"No," said Priya. "It's a *biography*."

Buddy's head was spinning.

"It doesn't matter what we decide," said Ms. Maple. "As long as we decide together. And we can put notes about the books in the other baskets. In case you forget where to look for them."

"Like a treasure hunt!" said Tamar.

Then it was Bea's turn. "My books," she said, holding them up, "are *Bea's Books*. They're books I want to read."

Ms. Maple paused. "I'm glad you found books you want to read," she said. Bea beamed. "*But*," said Ms. Maple. "I'm afraid we don't have enough baskets for everyone to have their own."

'No problem," said Bea. "I'll do a *double* basket. *Bea's*

Books and Some of Buddy's." She tried to grab Buddy's books out of his hands. He held them tightly.

"Bea," said Ms. Maple. "I don't think we can have baskets for individuals. What if someone else wants to read the books in your basket?"

"Then I'll *lend* them," said Bea. "Because it's a *library*. But they have to give them back."

Bea stuck her basket under her T-shirt. As if she were hiding it. But everyone could see it. It made a big bulge under her shirt. "I'll put notes in other baskets," she said. "So Tamar can do her treasure hunt."

Ms. Maple looked as if she were about to argue. But she pursed her lips. And moved on. "Buddy," she said. "What are your books?"

"Well," said Buddy. "They both have boys." He held up the books so everyone could see.

"And what category are you suggesting?"

"Is there a superhero basket?" asked Buddy.

"Those guys aren't superheroes!" said Priya.

Buddy didn't actually care which basket the books went in. As long as they weren't in the basket for *Bea's Books*. "*Books about Friends*, then," he said, which was the basket Marisol and Tamar were working on.

"Are there friends in the books?" asked Marisol.

"No," said Buddy. "But *the books* are friends." He waggled one. Then the other. And made them talk. "We're friends," he said in a funny voice. He looked back up. "See?"

"That's not what the category means," said Tamar.

Buddy hugged the books to him. "Can I keep them a little longer?" he asked. "Because, actually, it's kind of like they're *my* friends."

"See?" said Bea. "Buddy needs his own basket, too!"

Finally, everyone finished their turns. Ms. Maple smiled. "You're all doing a good job," she said. "Discussing the books. And listening to each other's ideas."

Buddy was glad to get a compliment. He raised his hand to give Ms. Maple one back. "And you did a good job, too," he said.

"Why, thank you, Buddy," she said.

"Because you are really, really good at making big messes!"

Ms. Maple laughed. "Well," she said. "Teachers have to be comfortable with a little bit of chaos."

"Sometimes a lot!" said Buddy.

Buddy was starting to feel better about being in Ms. Maple's class. At least a little. It was good that she liked messes. And also, she was sneaky.

Maybe at recess, he would tell the other kids. The kids in *Jabari's* class. Maybe then they'd wish they were in Ms. Maple's class.

Like he sort of still wished he was in Jabari's.

It wouldn't be like bragging, exactly.

Well, maybe it would be like bragging.

But just a little.

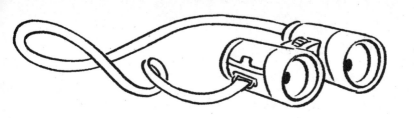

CHAPTER FOUR
Thinking Caps

That day, on his way to lunch, Buddy stopped short. He realized he was carrying those two books he liked. Whoops. He'd forgotten to leave them in the classroom.

But that was okay because Ms. Flores was walking toward him. So maybe it was lucky he had the books. He could show her how he made them talk to each other. This time, he used a deep superhero voice. "We're saving the world!" he said. Ms. Flores laughed.

Buddy still had to return the books to the classroom. Which made him even more late to lunch. By the time he finally got to the cafeteria, his friends were already leaving for recess.

Buddy ate quickly. Then he hopped up and ran to join them.

"Walk!" called a teacher.

It was Jabari. He had his binoculars. He was showing them to Cosmo, a kid in his class. "Want a peek?" he asked Buddy.

Buddy peered through. Everything looked a little blurry. But things always looked a little blurry around Jabari. Because he was so cool. Buddy was too flustered to ask how to fix the focus. Did Jabari remember what Bea had said? That Buddy wished he was in his class?

"Hey," said Cosmo. He reached for the binoculars. "These are for *our* class." Cosmo could be kind of annoying. "For when we go *bird-watching*."

Buddy felt like saying, "Who cares?" But Jabari was there. So Buddy said, "Well? We have *a mess* in *our* classroom."

Yikes. That didn't come out right. If he was going to brag, he'd need to come up with a better brag than that.

Buddy handed the binoculars back and headed out to the playground. Bea was already there. A crowd of kids was around her. Kids from Class 2–110, Jabari's class. Everybody knew Bea. Even though she was new at school, Bea was fast all right!

"Guess what," she was telling them. "This morning our class was a *pigsty*! It looked like a *tornado* whirled through it."

Somehow it sounded better when Bea said it. Bea was a better bragger.

"It blew the books all around," she was saying. "And now we have to sort every one. Even the crummy books nobody wants to read!"

Cosmo and Jabari had followed Buddy outside. Jabari

pointed to his class. "Hey!" he said. "2–110! Don't forget. Keep those thinking caps on!" Then he wheeled on his heel and walked back into school.

"Thinking caps?" said Bea. "Why do you need thinking caps?"

"None of your *BEA*swax," said Cosmo.

But another kid from 2–110 answered. "Because we're supposed to be thinking of a name," she said. "For our class."

"A name?" said Buddy. "But you already have one. 2–110. Jabari just said it."

"No," said Cosmo. "A *real* name. Not a plain old number. Because we're cool. The coolest class. So we need a cool name to match."

After recess, when they got back to their classroom, Buddy's class mobbed Ms. Maple. They were all talking at once.

"They're getting a *name*," said Joey.

"A *cool* name," said Malik.

"So *we* need a name," said Omar.

Ms. Maple stepped back. "Whoa," she said. "One at a time."

"We need a *real* name," said Bea. "Not a plain old number. Like 2–108."

Ms. Maple blinked. She looked confused. "A name for...?"

"Our *class*," said Buddy. "Jabari's class is getting one. So everybody will know how great they are."

"Oh," said Ms. Maple. She nodded. "A class name. Well, having a name could be fun. We'll just have to think of possibilities. And then vote."

"Ours has to be the best," said Buddy.

"Better than theirs," said Amber.

"We can't let them win!" said Bea.

"Win?" said Ms. Maple. "Are you thinking of this as a competition?"

"No," said Bea. "A *contest*."

Ms. Maple cocked her head. "We're not trying to *beat* Jabari's class," she said.

No one said anything. Because, actually, they all were.

As soon as Ms. Maple turned her back, Bea whispered. "We've got to *win!*" Everyone nodded. They all agreed.

They even put their hands together in the center. To make a pact.

"Game on!" said Joey.

Ms. Maple flipped open her big pad of paper. To write down their suggestions for class names.

Amber came up with the Studious Students.

"Too plain," said Bea.

Keiko suggested the Rainbow Unicorns.

"Too flowery," said Malik.

Tamar suggested the Bookworms.

The whole class groaned.

Then Bea suggested Team Tornado. She stood up and whirled around. Her arm banged into Buddy's head.

"Ouch!"

"It's good," said Priya. "But not best. I bet Jabari's class will think of something better."

Buddy couldn't think of any suggestions himself. Not even one. Coming up with a name was hard. A lot harder than he'd expected.

It was time to go to the tables and do other work. Buddy scuffed to his place. He wondered if Jabari's class was having a hard time coming up with a name, too. He

RAINBOW UNICORNS BOOK WORMS TEAM TORNADO

hoped so. Though, probably for them it was easy. Maybe a bird would swoop down. And drop a name right in their laps. It seemed to Buddy that actually might happen.

Jabari's class was lucky like that.

CHAPTER FIVE
The Rhymerinos

During math, Buddy finally thought of a name. The Number Ones!

Eesh. That sounded too much like a bathroom thing.

During science, he thought of the Scientific Observers.

Nah. That sounded like some movie his dads would make him watch.

When the class went back to sorting books, Buddy and his friends swapped suggestions.

"How about the 2–108 Gang?" said Joey.

"Too much like our old name," said Priya.

"What about the Rockets?" said Malik.

"Too, um . . . *rocket-y*?" said Omar.

"Hey," said Kaveh. "How about the Best Second-Grade Class? Too braggy?"

"We *need* to be braggy!" said Bea. "That's the whole point!"

There were still a lot of books left to sort. Everyone worked quietly for a while. Sorting and thinking. Sorting and thinking.

Suddenly, Bea cried out, "I've got it!"

"*Not* Team Tornado," said Keiko.

"No!" said Bea. "Better." She did a boppy little happy dance. "The Rhymerinos!"

"The Rhymerinos?" said Buddy. That was a weird name. "How did you even come up with that?"

Bea smiled mysteriously. "It just came to me. I think rhyming is really important, don't you?"

"Random," said Keiko. She went back to sorting. "Hey." She held up the poetry basket. It was nearly empty. "I filled this basket already. Where did all the books go?"

Malik was looking through the nature basket. It was crammed full, with extra books stacked on top. "And how'd this basket get so stuffed?" He pulled out some books. "A lot of these don't even belong."

Omar picked up the basket for graphic novels. "And

why are there poetry books in here?" he asked. "They *definitely* don't belong."

Was this another book mystery? Like when they'd found the books scattered around the classroom?

"Who did this?" asked Joey. He looked at their teacher.

"Not me," said Ms. Maple. "Not this time."

Bea was smiling a weird, crooked smile. "Probably it could've been a tornado," she said. "Or . . ." Now she was grinning wildly. "A Rhymerino!"

"You!" said Joey, pointing at her. "*You* did it!"

"*Somebody* had to fix the baskets," said Bea.

"*Fix* them?" said Keiko. "You messed them up!"

"Because," said Bea. "A lot of the books in the poetry basket didn't belong. They didn't *rhyme*. So I had to switch them."

Keiko, angry, crossed her arms across her chest. "Poems don't have to rhyme."

"Yes, they do," said Bea.

"No, they don't," said Keiko. "We learned that last year."

Now Bea looked angry, too. "Well," she said, "I learned

something in *my* school last year, too. And that's that poems always rhyme." She turned to Ms. Maple. "Right?"

"Poems *can* rhyme," said Ms. Maple.

"See!" said Bea.

"But they never have to," Ms. Maple added.

Bea sulked. "In my old school," she said, "we didn't even put books in baskets. We had a *library*. A real one."

"Bea," Ms. Maple said gently, "it's hard to be new, isn't it? It must feel strange to be doing things differently this year, differently from your old school."

"Yeah," said Bea. "Because this school does things *wrong*."

Malik fished a bunch of poetry books out of the nature basket. He handed them back to Keiko. Bea snatched one off the top.

"Hey," she said. "Look! A book about *birds*!"

"*Poems* about birds," said Keiko.

"I think we should give it to that other class," said Bea. "Because they like birds so much."

Ms. Maple considered. "You mean Jabari's class?" she said. "Well, that could be a friendly gesture, couldn't it?"

Buddy held his breath. Was Ms. Maple going to give something to the other class? To their *rivals*? Just to make Bea feel better?

"What do the rest of you think?" she asked.

No one said anything. Buddy knew why. Because no one wanted to look mean in front of their teacher.

"Bea," said Ms. Maple. "Would you like to bring the book to them? As our ambassador?"

"Yeah," said Bea. "And Buddy can go with me." She pulled Buddy up before he could block her.

He yanked free.

Bea leaned close to him. Was she going to spit? In his *ear*?

He jerked away. "No spitting!"

"I'm not," said Bea. "I'm *whispering*. Because I have something to *tell* you."

She tugged him out the door. "I have a plan," she said.

A plan? Bea always had a plan.

"Come on," she said. "I'll tell you outside."

CHAPTER SIX
Spies!

In the hallway, Bea didn't have to whisper. She told Buddy her plan. "We're going to Jabari's class so we can be *spies*," she said.

"Spies?" said Buddy.

"Yeah. We're on a mission. To get information. About their *name*."

Oh. That was interesting. Sometimes, Bea actually had good ideas. Buddy slowed down. And walked stealthily. Like a spy. They were heading into enemy territory.

The door was open.

"Friends!" Jabari greeted them. "From 2–108! Welcome!"

"We're not friends," said Bea. "We're *embarrassed doors*."

Buddy elbowed her. "Ambassadors," he corrected her.

Bea thrust the bird book toward Jabari. "Here," she

said. "We brought you this. Because you guys love birds so much."

"Why, thank you, Bea," said Jabari. "We can put this in our special basket. For bird books."

"You have a special basket?" asked Buddy. "Just for bird books?"

"We do," said Jabari. "We love to learn about birds."

Jabari showed them the basket. Buddy flipped through. There were a few books about bird identification. And one about migration. Plus a biography of a scientist who studied birds.

Bea poked Buddy's arm to remind him why they were there. *Spies*, she mouthed. She jerked her head toward the whiteboard at the other end of the room. There was a list there. Of names for the class. Every name had something to do with birds.

The Awesome Owls   The Cool Crows

The Flying Finches   Warbler Whiz Kids

The Squab Squad   The Bird Brain-iacs

"Um," Bea asked Jabari. "Did you guys choose a name yet?"

"Not yet," said Jabari. "We're still looking for one that describes us perfectly."

Buddy pulled another book out of the basket. It looked homemade. On the cover was a photo of a bird that was blue. It had a big, puffy crest on its head. "What's this book?" he asked. He read the title. "*Steller's Jay?*"

"Oh," said Jabari. He leaned closer. As if he was about to say something private, something just for Buddy and Bea to hear. "I made that when I was a kid. I was visiting my uncle out west. And I saw this bird. It kept following me. And squawking. Jays can be quite loud. So I made a book about it. It's the bird that got me started as a bird-watcher."

Buddy opened the book. Inside was a photo of Jabari when he was a kid. He had binoculars around his neck.

A familiar feeling washed over Buddy. The feeling of wanting to be in Jabari's class. He put the homemade book back in the basket. Then Jabari added the book Buddy and Bea had brought and thanked them for being good neighbors.

Bea nudged Buddy. "And good *spies*," she whispered.

On the way back to their class, Bea reached under her T-shirt. She pulled something out. It was the book they'd been looking at. Jabari's book about the bird.

Buddy stopped in his tracks. She hadn't.

"Ooh," said Bea. "Look." She paged through. "This bird is really pretty. I love birds that are blue." She traced her finger across the title, *Steller's Jay*. "Even its name is fancy."

"You *stole* Jabari's book?" said Buddy.

"I didn't steal it," said Bea. "I *borrowed* it. That's what the baskets are *for*."

"Yeah, but for *their class*."

"They should share," said Bea.

"Everyone will know you took it," said Buddy.

"You took it, too."

"Me?" said Buddy. "I did not!"

"But you're *my buddy*," said Bea. "And what one buddy does, the other does, too. It's the Buddy Rule."

"*We're not buddies!*" yelled Buddy. "And I never even heard of that Buddy Rule!"

Buddy grabbed Bea's arm. He tugged on it. He knew he wasn't supposed to. But sometimes? With Bea? He forgot. He tried to pull her back toward Jabari's classroom. "You have to put it back!"

Bea yanked away. "Let go!" she said. "Who wants to be your buddy anyway? You're a *bad* buddy. I thought you wanted to be a spy!"

"I *was* a spy!" said Buddy. "I don't want to be a stealer!"

"A *stealer*?" said Bea.

"I mean a *thief*," said Buddy. Sometimes, with Bea, he got so flustered, he even forgot the right words.

Bea puckered her face. "Are you going to tattle on me?"

Buddy didn't like to tattle. So he probably wouldn't. "I might," he said.

Bea huffed. "All right." She turned on her heel to go back to Jabari's room. She crept up, hugging the wall. Then she kissed the book. "I love you, little bluey bird," she said.

"You're slobbering on it!" said Buddy.

Slowly, sneakily, Bea reached around the doorway. Just her arm. She set the book back inside.

After that, Buddy and Bea ran until they got back to Room 2–108. They shut the door behind them.

Ms. Maple walked toward them, smiling. "Did you give them the book?" she asked.

"Yeah," said Buddy. "They put it in their bird basket."

"Oh," said Ms. Maple. "They have a basket just for bird books?"

"Everything in their class is birds," said Bea. "Even all the names on their list. That whole place is birds. Birds, birds, birds."

Buddy thought of a question for Ms. Maple. He'd wondered it before. But he kept forgetting to ask. "Are you going to take us tree-watching?" he asked.

"Tree-watching?" she said.

"Yeah. Like Jabari's class goes bird-watching. But you're Ms. *Maple*. So maybe we could study trees. Instead of birds."

Ms. Maple cocked her head. "That's an interesting idea," she said. "We could start by making a new basket. For tree books."

Yes! Everyone got busy. Looking for books for the basket. Though there wasn't much time left. The day was almost over.

While they were searching, someone knocked on the door. It was Cosmo.

"Jabari wants your class to visit," he said. "Now."

"Now?" said Ms. Maple. "All of us?"

"Yeah," said Cosmo. "We came up with our name."

A name? That was impossible. How could they have done that so fast?

"We're going to make a big announcement," said Cosmo. He pumped his fist. "'Cause we rule!"

CHAPTER SEVEN
The Stellar Js

Buddy walked to the other class with his friends. He was confused. How had Jabari's class thought of a name already? "They didn't have one yet," he told his friends. "Jabari said."

"Maybe a little birdie told them," joked Joey.

When they got to the classroom, Jabari was at the whiteboard, smiling broadly. He beckoned everyone near. He'd draped a scarf over the whiteboard to hide it. "Ready?" he said. "Ta-da!" He pulled off the scarf. Like a big reveal.

Now there was a picture of a bird there. That squawky blue bird. Underneath it was a name. Stellar Js.

"Wait," said Buddy. "You picked the name of that bird you liked? The one in your book?"

"Close," said Jabari. "That bird's name is similar. Steller's Jay. And it inspired us. So we came up with a name that sounds something like it: *the Stellar Js.*"

"Yeah," said one of the kids in his class. "*Stellar* 'cause we're stars. And the *J* part stands for Jabari. Because we're his Js. Our class is."

"It happened by accident," said Jabari. "A *happy* accident. The class had completely forgotten about that bird. But then Cosmo noticed my book."

"Yeah," said Cosmo. "It was supposed to be in the basket. But I found it by the door. How did it even get over there?"

Buddy stared accusingly at Bea.

"It was like a *sign*," said Cosmo. "To make sure we'd see it. So we could come up with the best name of all. The Stellar Js!"

All the kids in Jabari's class cheered. Everyone from Ms. Maple's class stayed quiet. Though, Joey murmured, "I guess a little birdie *did* tell them."

Buddy stomped over to Bea. He stuck his face close to hers. His *angry* face. "This is your fault!" he said, half hissing, half whispering.

"Nuh-uh," she said. "It's yours."

"Mine?" said Buddy. "*You're* the one who took the book."

"Yeah," said Bea. "But you're the one who made me put it back. If I'd kept it, Cosmo wouldn't have found it. Then he never even would've *thought* of that stupid name."

Bea stuck out her tongue at Buddy.

Really? She stuck out her *tongue*? Like in *preschool*?

Buddy stuck his tongue out back.

The other kids from their class had crowded around Jabari. He was showing them his book.

"You made that?" said Joey. "Really?"

"I did," said Jabari. "When I was around the same age as you guys."

"Wow," said Amber. "It's so cool."

Tamar sighed. "Stellar Js," she said. "It really is the best name." But she said it like it was a sad thing. Because for 2–108, it kind of was.

After the big reveal, the kids from 2–108 slogged back to their classroom.

"Now we really have to come up with a good name," said Amber.

"Better than the Stellar Js," said Marisol.

"We definitely have to beat them," said Bea.

The class straggled to the rug. It was nearly time to go home. Buddy thought of what the kids in Jabari's class had said when they'd announced their name. *The J part stands for Jabari. Because we're his Js.*

"Hey," he said. "That's it! They're Js because they're *Jabari's class*, right? But we're *Ms. Maple's*. So our name should be about *maples*!"

"*Stellar* idea," said Ms. Maple. She winked at Buddy. His face flushed.

"How about the Maple Rockets?" asked Malik.

Omar frowned. "What do *rockets* have to do with *maples*?"

"Nothing," said Malik. "I just want a name with *rocket* in it."

Kaveh had a suggestion, too. "The Mighty Maples."

"It's good," said Amber. "But probably not as good as the Stellar Js."

"Unfortunately," said Ms. Maple, "it's already time for dismissal. But I'm going to give you homework for the weekend."

Homework? Over *the weekend*? Everyone groaned.

"The homework is to think of names," said Ms. Maple. "*Maple* names. When we come back on Monday, we'll see what you've come up with."

Buddy was glad the school day was over. And he was even gladder it was the weekend. That would give them more time to brainstorm.

On his way out of school, Buddy ran into Cosmo. Cosmo pumped his fist again. "Stellar Js!" he chanted. Like he was cheering on his class. Like they were some kind of team. One that was *winning*.

"Yeah?" said Buddy. "So? We're going to have a name, too."

"Right," said Cosmo. "Good luck with that."

Though, Buddy could tell he meant the opposite.

CHAPTER EIGHT
Maple Syrple

There! Buddy sat at his table at home. He had just put the finishing touches on his project. It looked pretty good, if he did say so himself. He'd made a book! A homemade one. Just like Jabari's!

True, the book was a little lumpy. And bumpy.

That's because Buddy had used real objects to illustrate it. Like leaves. And a seed. He'd gotten the idea to make the book earlier in the day, when he and Poppy and Daddo had gone to the park. He'd collected leaves from a maple tree. And a maple seed, which didn't look like a regular seed. It had two little wing thingies coming off it. And it was super delicate. So it had been tricky to paste down. Buddy got a piece of tape, an extra-long one, to hold it better.

He held up the book and admired the cover. He'd written the title in big, careful letters.

BUDDY'S MAPLE TREE BOOK

"I'm an author!" he cried.

"You are," said Daddo.

"Great work!" said Poppy.

Buddy couldn't wait to show his friends.

On Monday morning, Buddy set the book beside him on the breakfast table.

Poppy flipped pancakes onto Buddy's plate. Buddy poured syrup on them. He got a few drops on the book. "Whoops."

"No worries," said Poppy. He helped Buddy blot it up.

"And anyway," said Daddo, "maple syrple goes with your maple theme."

"Maple *syrple*?" Buddy repeated. "Is that a word?"

"Not a real word, exactly," Daddo admitted. "But *syrple* sounds a little like *maple*. So it's fun to say."

Maple syrple. Buddy rolled the words around on his tongue. He downed his pancakes. And packed his book in his backpack.

At school, Bea ran up to him. She showed Buddy a book she and Amber had made.

"Wait," he said. "You made one, too?" They'd been inspired by Jabari's book, just like he had.

"We made it *together*," said Bea. She clapped her arm around Amber's shoulders. "Because Amber's my buddy now, too. You're not my only friend, you know."

Bea kept staring at him. Did she want him to say something? He didn't know what to say. Maybe, *That's good*?

He probably shouldn't say that.

He almost did.

Luckily, Ms. Maple called everyone to morning meeting. She wanted to hear their suggestions for class names.

The Maple Branches?

No.

The Magic Maples?

Better. But just a little.

"The Maple Staples," suggested Bea.

What? That didn't even make sense. It just rhymed.

"That's plenty of names," said Bea, dusting off her hands to move on. "So now I can show you the book I made."

"Book?" said Ms. Maple. She looked confused. Bea told

her about the homemade books she and Amber and Buddy had brought in. "What a lovely idea," said Ms. Maple. "We can put them in our tree basket."

Bea even let Buddy show his book first. Then she and Amber showed theirs.

"We went to a park," said Bea. "To look for animals."

"Animals?" said Buddy. "That's not trees."

"Animals who *live in* trees," said Bea. "Like squirrels and birds. And bugs."

"Our book is called *Tree Friends*," said Amber.

"And I saw a *special* tree friend," said Bea. "A hawk. It caught a rat. And then it *ate* it. And I learned this: there are all kinds of tree friends. And some tree friends eat other tree friends."

Ms. Maple had brought in a book for the tree basket, too. Though, hers wasn't homemade. It was a book about how trees talk to each other, to help each other grow.

"Wait," said Bea. "Trees talk? When? When we're asleep?"

"They don't talk like we do," said Ms. Maple. "But they communicate. They send messages to each other. Chemical messages. Through an underground web of connections. That link their roots."

"Messages?" said Bea. "You mean like *spy* messages?" She glanced at Buddy. She made her eyes wide. She mouthed, *Spies!*

"More like sharing information," said Ms. Maple. "For instance, if bugs are attacking. They send an alert. *Beware!*"

"Like an emergency alert," said Joey. "On the phone."

"Good comparison," said Ms. Maple. "And they also send food. To the trees who aren't getting as much."

Bea was starting to fidget. She reached over to grab Buddy's book. "Yuck," she said. "It's sticky."

"I got a little syrple on it," said Buddy.

"Syrple?" said Bea.

"Maple syrple."

"That's not a word," said Bea.

"But it's fun to say," said Buddy. "Right?"

Bea said it slowly, trying it out. "May-pul syr-pul. Yes!" She clapped her hands. "That's it! The perfect name for us! The Maple Syrples! And it rhymes!"

"It doesn't rhyme," said Keiko.

"It's our name!" said Bea. "It's decided!"

"Hold on," said Ms. Maple. "It's an interesting suggestion, but we still have to vote."

Bea waved her arms at the class, like a conductor cuing an orchestra. "All in favor?"

"Wait," said Priya. "I have a suggestion, too."

"You're too late," said Bea.

"I am not. I want to show this first," said Priya. She had something in her hand. "Like you showed your book."

Priya was holding one of those little maple-seed thingies.

"This," she said, "is a seed. From a maple tree. As you can see, it has wings."

Buddy frowned. "We already saw one of those," he said.

"In my book." Was Priya going to give them a *lecture*? Like a *teacher*?

"When the seed breaks away from the tree," Priya went on, "it flutters down. The wings help the seed travel far."

"Excuse me," said Bea. "But that is not a name. We're voting. Right now!"

Priya ignored her. "The real name of these winged seeds," she said, "is samaras."

"*SAM*-a-ras?" said Bea. "That's a terrible name! Nobody could even remember that!"

"*But*," said Priya, "they're also called . . ." She paused for effect. "Whirligigs."

A gasp waved through the class. Then a murmur. Everyone repeated the word. *Whirligigs.*

Now *that* was a word.

"The wings have a really good design," said Priya. "For spinning. They're wider at the bottom. So the air moves faster there. The wings create a tiny tornado."

Bea's mouth dropped open. "A tiny *tornado*?"

"So my suggestion for a name," said Priya, "is the Tiny Tornado Whirligigs!"

"But it doesn't say *maple*," said Malik.

"So?" said Priya. "It's about maples. Maple *seeds*."

"Whirligig," repeated Buddy.

"That word tastes sweet," said Bea. "Like syrple."

After that, nobody had any more suggestions. Everybody just wanted to vote.

Ms. Maple counted. She looked up and announced, "Every single vote is for . . ." She paused. Everyone waited. "The Tiny Tornado Whirligigs!"

"I won!" cried Priya.

"*We* won," said Bea. And everybody knew what she meant by that. That their class had beat Jabari's class.

"But," said Ms. Maple. "That name is a bit long. So I hope nobody minds if I shorten it when I call you. I'll probably just say *Whirligigs!*"

"Don't worry," said Bea. "We can take care of the tornado part!" She popped back up and started spinning. Joey made spinny hands and a dizzy face. Buddy and his friends whirled around Joey.

"Whirligigs!" everyone shouted.

Buddy couldn't wait to tell the Stellar Js.

He especially couldn't wait to tell Cosmo.

CHAPTER NINE
Seeds in the Tree

At recess, Buddy ran right out. "We're the Whirligigs!" he said, twirling around.

Bea ran, too. She whirled through a knot of kids, scattering them. "The *Tiny Tornado* Whirligigs!" she said. "Oops!" She knocked into a few.

Priya had brought her whirligig out with her. To show the Stellar Js. And tell them about the winged seeds.

"This," she said, starting her lecture, "is a seed. From a maple tree."

Cosmo grabbed it out of her hand. He snapped off the wings and pretended to munch them. "*Num, num, num!*"

"No!" cried Priya.

Buddy watched the fragile pieces of wing fall to the

ground. Cosmo spit some out. *Yuck!* Had he actually tried to *eat them*?

"Ha!" said Cosmo. "I! AM! BIRD! And BIRD! DESTROYS! SEED!"

And that's when it hit Buddy. He didn't want to be in Jabari's class. Not if Cosmo was in it. He didn't really like being around Cosmo at all.

Suddenly, everybody was yelling. And fighting. It happened really quickly. Buddy wasn't sure who yelled first. Or who yelled back. Or who pushed, or pushed back.

Push! Pull!

Yikes! Youch!

The fight surprised Buddy. It surprised *everybody*. Two playground monitors ran over to separate the classes. They sent the Stellar Js to one end of the playground. And banished the Whirligigs to the other.

Buddy and the other Whirligigs hunkered together underneath a tree. It wasn't much of a tree. It was scrawny. And scrappy. Its roots bulged out of the concrete. Like knuckles. Buddy squeezed miserably between two bony knobs.

Bea scrambled to sit next to him. Buddy angled away so he could ignore her.

Buddy and all the Whirligigs were quiet. A stunned quiet. Like, *What-in-the-world-just-happened?* At the end of recess, when Ms. Maple arrived to collect them, nobody even stood up.

"Whirligigs?" said Ms. Maple. "Is something wrong?"

"We had a fight," said Amber. "Kind of."

"Maybe I sort of pulled Cosmo's hair," said Priya. "Just a little." Whoa. Priya liked to tattle. But this time she was tattling *on herself?*

"They crumbled our whirligig," said Amber.

"Destroyed it," said Priya.

"Oh," said Ms. Maple.

"Sometimes it's hard to get along," said Buddy.

"A lot of the time!" said Priya. "Especially with Cosmo."

"Yeah," said Bea. She waved her arm. It bumped Buddy's head. "It's too easy to get into fights!"

"I know what you mean," said Ms. Maple.

"You do?" said Buddy. He rubbed the bumped part of his head.

"We have a lot of different personalities in our class. And that can be challenging."

"And there are even *more* personalities in the Stellar Js," said Buddy. "And some of them are challenging, too."

"*Really* challenging," said Priya.

"Agreed," said Ms. Maple. She waited a long time before saying anything more. Then she said, "Whirligigs?"

A small smile curved Buddy's lips. Whirligigs. It was a good name. A *winning* name. Even if Cosmo *had* eaten the seed.

"Right now," said Ms. Maple, "you're all like little whirligig seeds high up in our tree. You're all up here together, holding on and enjoying the branches. At some point, when you get bigger, a wind will come along. And it will blow you to new places. You'll spin. You'll glide. You'll fly."

"We'll make tiny tornadoes!" said Bea.

"You will," said Ms. Maple. "Of course, each one of you is a little bit different. But right now you're all maple seeds in this tree we share. So it's a time we can enjoy. Together. What do you think, Whirligigs? Can we do this together?"

Buddy liked the way she put it. He was glad he was a

Whirligig. He was in the best class. The best class for *him*. "But what about the Stellar Js?" he asked.

"Maybe they can be our friends," said Amber. "Because we're trees, and they're birds. You know. Sort of like *Tree Friends*."

"Exactly," said Ms. Maple. "They need us, and we need them."

"But *they ate the whirligig!*" said Priya.

"Because some tree friends eat other tree friends," said Bea.

The Whirligigs headed back into school. They passed Ms. Flores. She waved and called to Buddy, "How's my best Buddy? Saving the world?"

Not exactly, thought Buddy. But he managed a smile.

At the door of their classroom, Bea tried to push in front of him. Buddy put out his foot to block her. Bea bumped him with her hip, knocking him out of the way.

"Hey!" said Buddy. "No pushing!"

"I wasn't," said Bea. "It was a hip bump!"

"Stop saying that!" said Buddy. "*Hip bump isn't even a thing!*"

Buddy looked around. Their classroom was still a little

messy. There were some books left to sort. The place didn't feel *fizzy* anymore. But it felt settled. Like home. Everyone in the class had been working hard. Together.

And getting into fights somehow. Together.

And feeling bad about it. Together.

Because they were all Whirligigs.

Together.

Bea started singing. Loudly. A song she made up then and there.

> *Whirligigs are in the tree*
> *In the tree*
> *In the tree*
> *Whirligigs are in the tree*
> *In the mighty maple!*

"Now," said Bea, "we don't just have a class name. We have a class song. Because I just made one for us!"

She poked Keiko. "And see?" she said. "It rhymes. Because songs have to rhyme."

"That didn't rhyme," said Keiko.

"It did."

"*Tree* and *tree?*" said Keiko. "Words can't rhyme with themselves."

Bea ignored her. "TINY TORNADOES!" she cried. Again, she swung her arm. And again, she managed to bonk Buddy.

Buddy tried not to mind. After all, he and Bea were now seeds together. Ms. Maple had said. Seeds in the tree. *Their* tree. To be a Whirligig, Buddy realized, you had to be comfortable with a little bit of chaos.

Though, just to be safe, he moved out of Bea's way.

Because he was a seed who didn't like to get banged up so much.

And Bea?

She was a Whirligig who needed a little extra room.

ACKNOWLEDGMENTS

It takes a lot of people to turn a manuscript into a book. Thanks to Agent Andrea, Editor Catherine, Designer Lily, Illustrator Kris, Copy Editor Jamie, and all the many people at Peachtree who've welcomed Buddy and Bea and given them a happy home.

Thanks also to my niece Phoebe, who reads the manuscripts to make sure they pass the kid-authenticity test. Phoebe's qualifications:

- √ She's a kid.
- √ She's a voracious reader.
- √ She once got locked in a bookstore at closing time because she was crouched in a corner, engrossed in a book. THAT'S CRED!

There were also many people, over many years, who *inspired* the Buddy and Bea books. Including: All of the kids in my class when I was a teacher; the kids I met when my son was in school; and all of the excellent teachers I've met along the way.

TRUE OR FALSE?

In this book, Ms. Maple takes all the books out of the book baskets so the kids themselves can sort them. Do I actually know a teacher who did that?

TRUE! I do!

Her name is Marjorie Martinelli, a creative—and very brave!—teacher!

ABOUT THE CREATORS

Jan Carr is the author of more than fifty books, including picture books and books in popular series. She has worked as a Head Start teacher, a book editor, a magazine editor at Sesame Workshop, and taught writing at The New School and School of Visual Arts. She lives in New York City, where she bikes, attends theater and ballet performances, and carts her compost to the farmers market. Visit her at *JanCarr.net*.

Kris Mukai is a cartoonist and writer who lives and works in Los Angeles. She has drawn illustrations for *The New Yorker* and the *New York Times*. She currently works as a writer at Cartoon Network and has written for *Adventure Time*, *Craig of the Creek*, *We Bare Bears*, and the *WBB* spin-off *We Baby Bears*. In her spare time, she monitors hawk nests in her neighborhood. See more of Kris's work at *HiKrisMukai.com*.

Check out **ALL** of
BUDDY AND BEA'S
adventures!

ISBN: 978-1-68263-534-6

ISBN: 978-1-68263-535-3